LISA,
THE SHELL-LESS TURTLE

WRITTEN BY
JAMES Y.
WILLIAMSON

ILLUSTRATED BY
TAMI BOYCE

To my daughter, Sofia.

Always be true to yourself,
and be brave in sharing your gifts of kindness
and empathy with the world.
Let your joyous and free spirit shine now and forever.
How great it feels to be shell-less!

Once upon a time, there was a turtle named Lisa.

Lisa was not like the other turtles because she was born without a shell on her back.

She was a shell-less turtle.

In fact, she was the only shell-less turtle in school.

Most of the time, being shell-less seemed like a good thing to Lisa.

She was very fast and light on her feet.

She was an excellent swimmer.

She was great at jump rope and hula hoop.

And she could dance and twirl and do cartwheels too!

But sometimes, Lisa wondered what it would be like to have a shell of her own like all the other turtles.

After all, they always had a place to hide if they were scared,

At school, other turtles would sometimes pick on Lisa and call her names.

"Shell-less Lisa!" they'd taunt.

"Forget your shell?" they'd laugh.

When the turtles said mean things, it made Lisa sad. Sometimes, it was hard being the only shell-less turtle in school.

Luckily for Lisa, she had good friends, Sheldon and Rochelle, who knew just what to say.

"Don't listen to them. Being shell-less is cool!" said Sheldon.

"Yeah, don't mind them! You don't need a shell to be fabulous!" said Rochelle.

Lisa felt much better and gave her friends a big hug. She DID feel fabulous, but she still wanted a shell of her own.

Then she had an idea.

"I know!" she said. "I'll build one! Will you help me?"

"Of course!" Rochelle said. "How fun!"

"When do we start?" Sheldon asked.

"First thing tomorrow!" Lisa replied. "But first, we need to do some research."

After school, the three friends went to the library and brought home a bunch of books about building your own shell.

They found a design they liked, gathered building materials, and promised to get together the very next day.

"Get some rest!" Lisa said. "We have a big day ahead of us."

The next morning, Lisa and her friends got to work.

First, they used clay to make the outer shell.

Next, they added a wooden frame inside the shell to make it extra strong.

And then they put comfy padding on the inside and some shoulder straps so that Lisa could wear her new shell like a backpack.

"All that's left now is the finishing touches," Lisa said.

"Finishing touches?" Sheldon and Rochelle asked at the very same moment.

"Oh yeah!" exclaimed Lisa. "I have bright colorful paints and decorations, and YOU'RE going to help me decorate!"

The three friends got busy, and before they knew it, the shell was finished!

GLITTER

GLITTER

PAINT

PAINT

PAINT

GLUE

"We did it!" Sheldon cheered. "This is the coolest shell I've ever seen."

"You finally have a shell that's as special and wonderful as you are!" Rochelle said, nearly tipping over with excitement.

Lisa jumped for joy. "Thank you so much! You're the best friends a turtle could ever have. I couldn't have done it without you," she said.

Lisa couldn't wait to wear her new shell to school the next day.

As soon as Lisa walked into the classroom, she received compliments from the other turtles.

"Wow, your shell is pretty cool!" said one.

"That shell is awesome!" shouted another.

Best of all, Lisa's teacher, Ms. Turtleton, loved her shell so much that she asked her to tell the class all about it during a special show and tell.

Lisa asked Rochelle and Sheldon to come up and join her.

The friends shared about how they worked together, first researching a design, then finding materials, and then building and decorating the beautiful shell that Lisa was wearing. The class and Ms. Turtleton were very impressed!

"Amazing!" said Ms. Turtleton.

"What a great invention!" said one of Lisa's other classmates.

"Do you have anything else to share with the class?" Ms. Turtleton asked.

"Yes, just one more thing," Lisa replied, as a broad grin appeared on her face.

"I used to think that I needed a shell to fit in," she continued. "But now I know that isn't true. What I learned from building this shell is that friendship is what's really important."

Lisa took off the shell and gave her friends another big hug. With her arms still around Sheldon and Rochelle, she turned to the class and yelled: "How great it feels to be shell-less!"

The whole class clapped and cheered as the three friends smiled and took a bow.

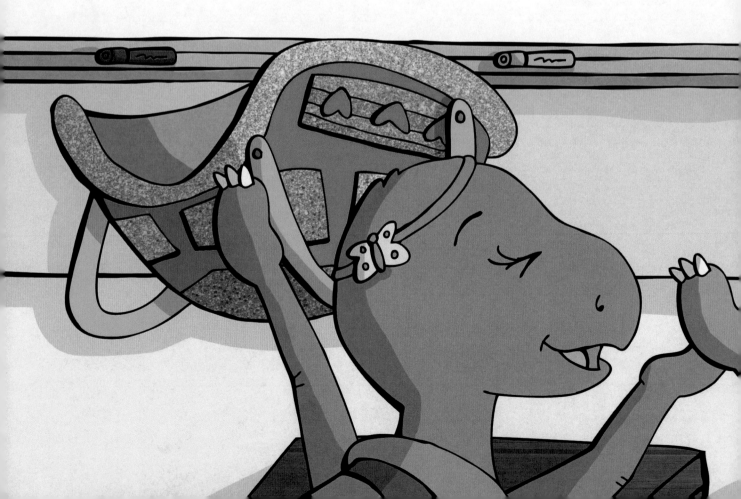

As the friends walked home
from school that day, Lisa
started singing a merry tune.
"Let's sing along together!"

"It's a sunny day. Come out and play.
How great it feels to be shell-less!

We have some fun and get the job done.
How great it feels to be shell-less!

A shell isn't as safe as it may seem.
We can do anything as a team!

How great it feels to be shell-less!"

THE END

MEET THE AUTHOR AND ILLUSTRATOR

James Williamson is a science writer and first-time children's book author based in Palo Alto, CA. When he's not writing, James enjoys spending time with friends and family, traveling, fly-fishing, and exploring the great outdoors.

Tami Boyce, an illustrator with a fun and whimsical style, is based in Charleston, South Carolina.

"Holding a pencil in my hand has been my passion for as long as I can remember. We live in a very serious world, and I like to use my quirky style to remind us of the love, joy, and humor that is often overlooked around us."

To see more of Tami's work, visit tamiboyce.com.

ACKNOWLEDGEMENTS

As Lisa and friends show us, "We can do anything as a team!" First and foremost, I'd like to give a special thanks to Tami Boyce who brought the Lisa story to life with her vibrant, whimsical, and heartwarming illustrations. Also, I'd like to thank Susan Burlingame for her outstanding copy editing help, and accomplished children's book author, Russ Towne, for mentoring me in the early stages of writing the story. Lastly, I'd like to thank my family for their unconditional love and support and for their creative input along the way.

Made in the USA
Middletown, DE
18 July 2020

13167727R00020